D0452881

Hansel, Gretel and the Ugly Duckling

Written by Hilary Robinson
Illustrated by Simona Sanfilippo

WAYLAND

LONDON BOROUGH OF HACKNEY LIBRARIES	
HK12000919	
Bertrams	26/06/2013
R PURPLE	£4.99
PURPLE	20/03/2013

"Hansel," said Gretel, "we have no food, and Dad needs more wood to make pegs. Let's walk to the farm down by the stream, and sell what we have for some eggs."

"We'll go through the forest," said Hansel, "and pick up some wood on the way. We'll buy some wheat to grind into flour and be back by the end of the day."

Hansel dropped stones to make a long trail
so they could find their way back.

Just as they got to the farm by the stream, they heard a little duck quack.

"Oh no!" cried Gretel. "Look at those ducks! They're teasing the one that is brown. They think he's not as handsome as them, and the ugliest duck in the town!"

"See how they leave him only the crusts,
while they eat the bread that is white.
And see how they snuggle up in the reeds,
while he sleeps alone through the night."

They bought grain and collected the wood,
and then they baked bread for their tea.

Father said, "Children, please can you go
and gather some woodchips for me."

This time they took bread for the ducks, and left a crumb trail as their guide.

But night time soon came and the
children got lost.
"Where will we sleep?" they both cried.

"Look over there in the trees," Hansel said.

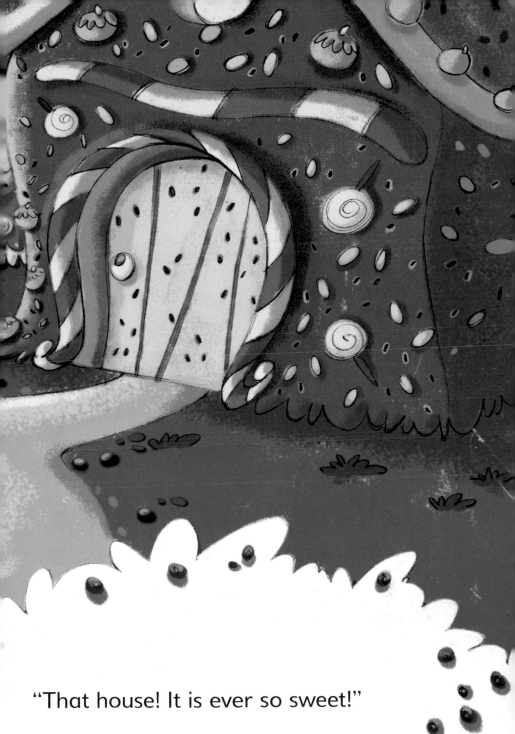

"That house! It is ever so sweet!"

"Do we dare go and knock on the door and ask for something to eat?"

Just at that moment a woman appeared. "Ha, ha!" she said. "Come with me!"

But as they stepped through the doorway,
she locked up and threw out the key.

The little duck had followed the trail,
and eaten the bread as he ran.

He saw the children trapped in the house, and he thought up a rescue plan.

When the old lady went to her bed, he picked up the key for the door.

He flapped his wings, flew up in the air,
and dropped it right on the floor.

"Hansel," said Gretel, "the duckling is here!
I can't believe what he's done!
He's brought us the key to help us get out.
Unlock the door and let's run!"

The children ran far away from the house with the duckling leading them on.
He lived the rest of his days on their pond and grew into a...

...beautiful swan!

START READING is a series of highly enjoyable books for beginner readers. **The books have been carefully graded to match the Book Bands widely used in schools.** This enables readers to be sure they choose books that match their own reading ability.

Look out for the Band colour on the book in our Start Reading logo.

The Bands are:

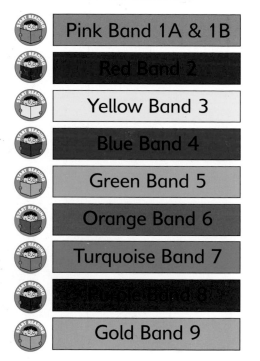

Pink Band 1A & 1B

Red Band 2

Yellow Band 3

Blue Band 4

Green Band 5

Orange Band 6

Turquoise Band 7

Purple Band 8

Gold Band 9

START READING books can be read independently or shared with an adult. They promote the enjoyment of reading through satisfying stories, plays and non-fiction narratives, which are supporte.d by fun illustrations and photographs.

Hilary Robinson loves jumbling up stories and seeing how they turn out. Her life is a jumbled up lot of fun, too! Hilary writes books for children and produces radio programmes for BBC Radio 2 and, because she really likes doing both, she really feels as if she is living happily ever after!

Simona Sanfilippo loves to draw and paint all kinds of animals and people. She enjoyed reading illustrated fairytales as a child and hopes you will enjoy reading these fairytale jumbles, too!